this poem is a house

ken sparling

Coach House Books, Toronto

first edition

Published with the generous assistance of the Canada Council for the Arts and the Ontario Arts Council. Coach House Books also acknowledges the support of the Government of Canada through the Canada Book Fund and the Government of Ontario through the Ontario Book Publishing Tax Credit.

LIBRARY AND ARCHIVES CANADA CATALOGUING IN PUBLICATION

Sparling, Ken, 1959-, author
    This poem is a house / Ken Sparling.

Issued in print and electronic formats.
ISBN 978-1-55245-334-6 (paperback).
    I. Title.

PS8587.P223P64 2016   C813'.54   C2015-908202-1

This Poem Is a House is available as an ebook: ISBN 978-1-77056-453-4 (EPUB), ISBN 978-1-77056-454-1 (PDF), ISBN 978-1-77056-462-6 (MOBI)

Purchase of the print version of this book entitles you to a free digital copy. To claim your ebook of this title, please email sales@chbooks.com with proof of purchase or visit chbooks.com/ digital. (Coach House Books reserves the right to terminate the free digital download offer at any time.)

§

God knew that all over the world people were thinking.
Old men cried thinking
back over their years of lament
and mistrust. It wasn't their fault.
God felt that people wanted him.

God was a technician.
He knew how to scrape away at the world.
He could encroach without rupturing.
He knew his job.

God didn't create the world at all –
he discovered the world
and then introduced it to the masses.
And now everyone holds him personally responsible.

§

The boy wanted to go out into the snow
and be flash frozen,
only to be found ten million years later,
a mythical beast, a symbol.
A dead one.

§

What place do we hold in ourselves for God
when God comes visiting
and our chests expand till they hurt,
God crushing the breath out of us
till our teeth blow out
of our faces like tiny white heat-seeking missiles.

We have seen the clouds.

§

Once upon a time there was a little boy and a little girl
who lived in different places
and didn't know each other.
Then they grew up and met each other
at a dance club.

The boy was attracted to the girl's curly hair,
crooked front teeth and wayward eye.
He soon fell madly in love with her.

Who are these people? the girl whispered
when they were together
on the dance floor.
I don't know, said the boy. *I've never met any of them.*
Tell me a story, said the girl.
The boy tried to look
the girl in the eye, but he couldn't tell

which eye
to look in.
Well, he said, finally, *in this story the girl felt*
that the boy was a walking fashion statement,
but even so, she spent time with him only because
she couldn't seem to get him to go away.

Each of the girl's eyes seemed to have its own mission.
The boy wanted to understand
the girl's mission
so he could address
the correct eye when he was telling her
his story.

§

The boy came across the bridge.
A crowd was waiting
on the other side.
He saw people.
People he knew.
He saw his mom.
He saw Mrs. Haversimmel.
Old Lady Rain.
Spot.

He felt lonely.

Step forward, they hissed.
They were angry
at him.

Seeing them made him sad.

They were disgusted.
Grow up! they told him.

But the boy was asleep
again and the people were gone
and the morning ravished him
and he got dressed
and went out
to the driveway
and stood with his heart bent forward
in his chest.
The light hurt his eyes.

His dad was suddenly there
beside him, lighting up a cigarette,
squinting into the morning.
He looked so tired.
He needed a shave.

The boy turned away into the hurting space
and tried to stare at the moment truthfully,
with no illusions.
His dad put the cigarette into his mouth,
drew on it
deeply.

§

When people talk, the boy told the girl, *I hear what they say*
but something that I want goes
beyond,
or somehow arrives
under the bright sky,
like hearing the secret pantings of a soul
whispering a secret message.

Who is God?
What is God?
If you ask the question
wrong, they say you will never get the answer
right. Most people already know
the answer they want,
so it's easy to get the question right.
It's harder when you really don't know.

§

The boy's boots made the girl feel
nervous. They were sitting
on the window ledge
in the bedroom. She didn't even know
for sure if they were the boy's boots.

Those aren't the boy's boots, she thought,
and it scared her,
the way the dark scared her, descending
as it did,
like a boot
coming

down
on
daylight.

The boots on the window ledge looked
like a pair of boots the girl had seen
on the boy's father's feet
in a picture that was pinned
to a bulletin board
at the funeral for the boy's father.
The girl wondered if the boy had kept the father's boots
squirrelled away all this time
in the back of a cupboard
in the house somewhere
where the girl would not find them,
the way he squirrelled away small items
of furniture,
like footstools and TV tables.

She imagined the boy's father in his coffin,
the boy leaning in,
taking the boots off his father.

She imagined the father now, in his coffin
in the ground,
in those long black socks
he used to pad around in
when they went to visit him
before he was dead.

§

I am afraid, the boy told the girl,
of what lies beyond, in the windy motion
on the plane where beams of light grow
hard against crisp night.

§

The boy wrote what mattered.
Then he wrote what didn't.
After that, there would be a moment
when he would no longer be capable
of writing
anything.

§

The tree had gone strange, the boy told the girl,
and when we looked at each other
we found we had the same wind on us
but a different wind, also,
each of us.

Because every speck of wind
coming down the hill that morning
was a different speck of wind,

yet they all came down the hill together
like they were going to a party
and not each to its own destiny.

I am rising in the wild windy dark.

§

Roll down your window, the boy said. *It's okay.*
The girl was afraid.
She spent a lot of time playing with the dogs.
The dogs were white.

The girl had feelings.
She tried to slip past them.

She tried to slip her feelings into random moments
of the alreadiness of her ongoing and uncooperative life,
as though they weren't her moments
but moments that belonged to another person,
as though they were on loan to her
from the library of moments.

§

The boy's dad died in October.
Christmas dinner that year was baloney
and honey.

§

These are people, the boy told himself.
These are people who have been riding Route 6
every night of their lives.

When the door opened
at the front to let people off, the lights came on.
It was like daylight.
It was like creation.
The guys who designed this bus sure knew a thing or two
about lights, the boy thought.

People on the closed highways were freezing
to death in their cars.

§

I was in the rec room today, the girl said. *Did I tell you
about that already?*
I have long wavy hair, she added at the last minute.
Then, more languorously: *I am a goddess, really,
in the looks department.
I should send you a picture.*

The boy wrote on medium-sized post-it notes,
which he left
on the fridge
for the girl
to find
to endear him to her
while he was locked away
in the basement

for the day,
making plans
to move the furniture
around the house.

Spike is our baby kangaroo, the boy wrote,
and he's inviting school kids to come
out for the festivities and to pay him
a visit.

§

The girl was in the attic. Piles of books
rose like apartment buildings. A wardrobe sat
at the back by a window. A child's dresser lay on its side
in the middle of the room. The girl was looking
for something, a book
the boy had told her about
a long time ago.
But after a while the girl forgot
what she'd come up
to the attic for and she stood
by the window
in the muted light, humming
a song.

§

The smoke from the girl's cigarette seemed
to have a dark purpose.
It curled richly around the conversation.
I don't smoke anymore, the girl said, exhaling smoke,
her chest falling like an avalanche.
But you make me nervous.

She was wearing a party dress
over a pair of ratty jeans.
Her feet were bare and wiggly.

Cigarette? She offered the pack.
I don't smoke, the boy managed.
You could start. The girl smiled. It was a mischievous smile.

§

They were all laughing
and drinking
wine.
The boy put his coat on
and went out
the front door
and walked to the end of the street.
It was his father's street
and his father was with him.
The snow was coming
down in big, fluffy flakes.
It was beautiful.

§

I believe in lying, said the girl,
down on white.
And, sure, red will arrive.
But lie
on your back
on the white
and let the red ride
over you like a lover.

The jello seahorses rode the waves of the bed
like they were starving.
They rode like stallions salivating
in the form of a new god.

White foam rode
over the edges
of the boy's dream
like white cum spilling
from the hole
at the top of a cock,
dripping like rain
being pushed
across a moving windshield.

There were amber anchors
in the sand.
A flotilla of boats rushing, suddenly leaving
the world behind.

Dripping gobs of humanity
ran over the far edges of the earth
drifting into the infinite vacuum,
sliding beneath the grand waterfall
at the far end of the great god's garden.

§

The girl pushed her face
into the place where the morning felt
most vulnerable. She watched the day
arrive
like a trigger
on a gun.

The boy was drifting around
the house on slippers, making notes
on scraps of paper, leaving them in places
around the house where he could locate them
later to help him try to find a path
through the chaos of his life.

It was like the boy had set his life down
one day and then forgotten where
he put it.

§

Someone thought
the morning might finally come,
the boy told the girl,
but Mother said no.
If anyone had a claim to the mountains,
it would be Bear, who we saw that summer
running over the world like spring water sprung.

The boy prayed mightily that the wind would let up,
and sometimes, yes, the trees would stop falling
and they would gather together in the calm,
amid the carnage,
shiny-eyed and hungry.

The boy's dog would live long
enough to see the river again.

I loaded things into my wagon, the boy told the girl,
and I pulled it out onto the road.
Pa stood on the porch and screamed
himself hoarse, but the wind took his words
and tossed them over the house
and I never heard a word
nor even the sound of his voice, again.
I turned once and saw Pa
with his mouth open
and that's the last I ever saw of Pa.

§

The angel was made of music. She floated
in and out
of the boy's life like he was locked out
of something,
a cathedral where a boys' choir practiced
the same two notes
over and over,
bridging sometimes into
variegated harmonies
that the boy couldn't quite grasp
till the girl came home
and folded her wings
around him like a cocoon,
making the boy feel
broken.

§

There was a spoon
that the boy kept
locked in a book
safe on a bookshelf
in the back room
behind the clothes
in the closet he'd set
near the portable washing machine,
next to where the dog house had been before
the boy carried it upstairs
and put it in the bedroom.

§

He would bring the girl
a chair that he'd been keeping
in the garage since the old man lived down there
for a week. Two more pieces of furniture to move –
since the old man was surely gone
for good – and he'd be able to put a car in there,
if they had one,
which they didn't.

The boy began to imagine
a bed in the garage.

The old man had slept
on a board
set over two sawhorses
with a couple of pillows on top.

One night the old man must have fallen off.
He came out in the morning bruised along one side
of his body.
It was a hundred degrees
and the old man was padding
around in his underwear
in the driveway
and the boy saw him
from the kitchen window.
He should put some clothes on, the boy thought.
The old man looked sad
and tired and one side of him was blue.
He must have fallen, the boy told himself.

I need to get him a proper bed.
Then, later
in the morning,
the boy had wrestled
his own bed
down the stairs and out
into the driveway. But then the garage door went up.
The old man was standing there blinking
in his boxers and
the boy realized just then that it wasn't going to work.
None of this was going to work.
The old man was never going
to agree to sleep in a bed.
It wasn't devious enough.
The boy needed to be more devious.
But the old man would always be more devious
than the boy and would out-think the boy
at every turn
because, really, the truth was, the boy did not want to think
anymore. He hauled the bed back up the stairs.

§

The girl had this way
of standing. Her weight on one foot. Looking
at the air beside her.
She did this now, in the middle
of the living room,
as the boy set his coffee on the edge
of the ottoman he'd brought
in from the hallway.

The girl looked
at the boy.
She was thin
as a wisp.
A child.
Beautiful.
Her motion.
The angle she maintained
above the ground.
Her grace.

Outside, through the window, the girl could see
shreds and snippets of smoky cloud that danced
their slow dance across the hazy sky
like dizzy birds.
The girl's eyes strained
and tore at the sky,
tried to pull it back
to her. She felt
as though she were doing
a painting, that she herself had created this sky.
I'll bring it with me, she whispered
wherever I go.

The girl cried.

This is what the boy had not expected.
Never in his life
could he have predicted
this.
He had not seen this coming.
Not any of it.
Not the clouds,

not the sky,
not the girl crying.

He sat the girl down in a chair,
asked if he could get her anything.

She cried
some more. Ran
the back of her hand over her eyes.

The boy opened a drawer
in the credenza
sitting next to them.
He'd put some Kleenex in there
a long time ago,
he remembered.
He reached in
the drawer and pulled
out CDs. Some tape. A stapler. A chocolate bar.
An empty aspirin bottle.

The girl laughed.

The boy got the Kleenex, finally.
He held the box
out to the girl.

§

There was light dusting the snow on the sidewalk
in front of the house and the boy and the girl were looking

out the big front window in the living
room. Now and then car headlights swept
a swathe through the falling white.
God's beard, the boy said.
The girl hooked her thumbs into the belt loops of her jeans.

I write because it makes me happy, the boy told the girl.
The boy left the girl
in the living room and went
to try to find some coffee.
He thought he might have left
the coffee maker in the rumpus room,
or maybe in the shed
out back.

§

The room at the back of the house
was where they kept things
they didn't know
what else to do with.

One time, the boy found his father
in that room, talking
to the angel.

§

The boy was sitting on a step
at the bottom of the dark stairway
that led up from the back room
to the second floor of a part of the house that had been torn
down by a previous owner.
The boy was playing a guitar
that the girl had brought home that morning
from a garage sale.
The music climbed
the stairway, echoed
off the door at the top, and rolled
back down, sometimes like thunder,
sometimes like gentle rain.

The boy played one last amalgamation
of notes, his hands twisted like creatures
in pain, then set the guitar down and climbed
the stairs to the door at the top, which opened
into empty space. There was a ladder
from the top of the stairs
down into the garden.

The girl was in the yard, under
a straw hat, wearing her white sundress
that ended
just below her knees. She was sitting
in a lawn chair, holding a glass
in her hand, a straw pinched
between two fingers as she sipped something pink.

When the boy opened
the door, she looked up and waved.

The boy climbed down the ladder.
Could you hear the music? he asked.
He set his hand on her
shoulder and let it rest
there.
Yes, said the girl. *It was muffled, like kittens
in a basket mewling
on the back of a bike.*
The boy smiled.
It was beautiful, said the girl.
The boy climbed back up the ladder,
went back into the house and
descended the stairs.

§

And then, one day, I was a kid,
said the boy. He and the girl were sitting
on a pile of blankets on the floor
of the bedroom
where the bed used to be.

Where is the bed? the girl asked.

But the boy continued
with his story. *And when I was a kid,
things could make me happy,* he said,
*and writing was what made me happy.
And the people I wrote for were happy.
They were happy*

that I wrote. And that is still the case
today.

I liked the bed, the girl said.

§

When you let go of the tree, you fall asleep.
The girl knew this to be true. It was her lullaby.

Where the boy was now was in sleep,
the sky still overcast,
but it would soon not be.
You could see where the clouds were going,
and where they were not going.
You could see how it would end,
and it was only a matter of time.
There would be a turning point,
and then time would begin, again,
to be worried about the positioning of the world
in relation to its own falling.

The boy was falling
from a tree.

§

There was a ladybug on my knee, the boy said.
He opened his eyes.
The girl was on her back,
in the bed
beside him. They were in the living room.
The boy turned his head to see the girl.
She looked like cream swirling
into coffee.

I flicked the ladybug away, said the boy.
The girl seemed to be asleep.
And it flew over the beach,
away from me,
toward the water.

It disappeared for a moment,
into the place where water meets shore,
then reappeared again, out over the water.

I tried to keep it in my vision.
I saw random spots
of black above the water.
One of the spots turned into a bird,
which dove into the water.
And when I woke, you were here beside me.

The girl sighed.

She doesn't care what I say, the boy thought.

She was listening only to the melody of his voice.
So he sang her a song of words without inflection,
words she could inhabit

with her own ideas,
and they would start out as black spots
on a papery dawn sky
and fly out into the world
where they would be greeted
by all the other words
out there
and the world would be a honeydew melon
where you trudged across the surface, trying to stay
on top of things.

§

It hurts to speak a single word,
to leave a word alone like that,
and the boy wants to pull it back
to safety, but
it's too late.
I'll have to be more careful, the boy thought.
And maybe he says some things the girl doesn't want
to hear.
And maybe he talks more than he ought to.

She wants to hear what he says
as a series of sentences
that become

a poem.

Like circus elephants letting go of each other's tails.

It seems
to the girl that the boy has got things
under control,
finally,
so she doesn't worry
about the furniture that is manifesting
in new locations all over
the house. She gets used
to turning on the lights
when she gets up at night to wander
the house so she doesn't run
into any stray furniture.

Lost furniture, she calls it.
The dresser dead centre of the living room.
The ottoman by the kitchen window.
The house is a poem,
she tells herself.

And the girl wants a story.
She still wants a story.
She hasn't given up on this.

But the boy seems calmer now, and the story
the girl tells can house the boy's poem,

maybe.

Maybe she can hold his poem safe
inside her story.

She can't abide, though, the terrible blinking
of her eyes when she turns on a light

in the middle of the night
when she goes to the living room to sit
on the couch and feel
deep inside herself
the effort of trying again to feel
what she might have never felt but hopes
she isn't just imagining.

So she carries a flashlight.
She keeps, always, a flashlight
on the table by the bed
by her head.

She tries a variety of flashlights
over the course of a week or two
and finally settles for the flashlight
app on her phone,
because it's so soft
as to be almost useless.
It almost doesn't serve its purpose.
She likes a thing that serves its purpose by almost falling
short
of serving
its purpose.
Like the boy,
she supposes.

§

The boy was playing
solitaire on a small table

that the girl had never seen
before. Every now and then the boy looked
up. *Where are we?* he asked the girl,
his eyes falling away from his question
like pebbles tumbling from a culvert after a rain
storm. He looks bewildered, the girl thought.
We're in our house, she said.
The boy saw a cat run
across the road
in front of the house.
The boy's hair was dishevelled, and the girl thought,
He looks like an old cat, himself.
The boy's cap lay on the seat
between them.
The seat was a green vinyl bench seat
that the boy had taken
out of an old school bus
and brought home one day
in the spring
of the first year
he and the girl were married.

§

The angel was brilliant. Not just in aspect, but in manner
as well. She shone. Her words were simple, ordinary,
but she had the face of an angel, and the boy found himself
drawn these days to the most ordinary
of language. It touched him
in places he didn't dare consider
in too much detail. Places that seemed outside

the reality of his body
and mind, like he had at some point become a part
of a confederation
of feelings that weren't exactly his but that he could feel
as keenly as though they were emanating
from the core of his being.

§

We should get a dog, the boy says.
No we shouldn't, says the girl.

§

Dogs never die
in the boy's mind's eye.

§

The boy loves the girl.
Seeing her sitting in the yard in her lawn chair,
with the towel over the back of her neck to keep it
from getting burnt.
And he loves her all the more for what she thinks she is
that she isn't.
He loves the girl he sees beneath the girl she sees.
He loves to try to look down her top.

He likes it when she's busy
reading a book
or eating her cereal
and he passes by
and tries to see down her top.

It makes him feel less alone.

He remembers turning into a teenager, that feeling
he always had.
It scared him sometimes,
but at other times it was like bliss spilling
out through his veins.
Like some kind of drug that got into every cell in his body
and made him feel like collapsing
on the spot
and quivering
on the floor
like some large sea creature beached
and baking in the sun.

But let's not get carried away here.

§

A poplar was shaking its shaggy head at the sky
in the early morning cold. It was September
and the girl was at a beach somewhere on a trip
with her mother.

The boy was on his back
on the floor of the living room, which was empty
of furniture now
that he'd moved it all out to the driveway.

Mother is still asleep in the cabin, the girl said to the boy.
The boy held the phone
to his ear and stared up at the ceiling.
He tried to imagine the cabin
they were staying in.
It would be made of wood, he thought.
White wood.
But that was as far as he got.

The girl had been able to capture a rare cellphone beam
that morning and gain reception
while standing on the beach alone
in the early morning light.
Usually, you have to be on top of the hill,
above the beach, to get reception, the girl told the boy.
But the air was so cold and still that I decided to go for it.
The girl told the boy that the cellphone beams must be
falling
out of the sky like supernovas selling starlight to Earthlings.
The boy asked the girl how long she'd been awake.
Two days, the girl said.
The girl didn't sleep as much as she used to.
She said she didn't need it, but when she'd been up
for a few days, she started talking
a certain way.
She saw trees with heads
and animals rooted to the soil.
It scared the boy, but it also elated him

to think there was this whole other world opening itself
to the girl like some kind of cornflower opening
its petals to the sun.
The girl continued to spout inadvertent poetry
while the boy lay on the floor alone
in the living room
with the phone pressed against his ear
like the girl's words were oxygen and his
ear was a nose.
It was like the girl was sprinkling seed deep
into the folds of another dimension,
one the boy could not see
but could feel in the tip of his being.
It was the dark undercurrent of a universe that made him,
when he thought too much
about it, unable to catch his breath.

§

The boy stepped out of his bedroom in his socks.
He squinted.
There was too much light
coming in
through the skylight.
He had no shirt.
His boxers had SpongeBob
smiling on them.
His socks were dark brown.
He went to the basement.
The girl was still asleep in bed upstairs.
It was the weekend.

The boy stood by the coffee maker for a while.
Then sat
on the blue chair
that was in the hall
by the washing machine.

They had too many chairs.

They got the blue chair when someone put it out
for garbage.
All of the chairs were in places around the house,
but the boy couldn't remember where most of them were.

The coffee maker beeped. The boy pulled himself
to his feet and poured
coffee into his mug.
Today, he was planning to move the dresser.
He would move the dresser to the landing
and start taking things out of it.
Meanwhile, the girl would be doing whatever
it was she did
on weekends.

The girl knew that everything
to do with the furniture was temporary.
Nothing was permanent
in the entire universe,
but knowing that did not help her deal
with the furniture
never being in the same place.
It bothered her in a way
she wished it didn't.

The boy took a sip
of his coffee, which was a light brown
from the cream
he put in. He stood by the coffee maker taking sips
of coffee.
He didn't want to move
away
from the coffee maker
too soon. It was the weekend
and there was no hurry.
He had all day.
He had only one plan.
He wanted to move the dresser.
And maybe look inside a few of the drawers.
He had no illusions.
He would not be looking in all the drawers.
He had no desire to look in all the drawers.
He would glance into only a couple of drawers.

He looked down at his boxers and beyond
to his socks. Otherwise he wouldn't have moved
away from the fridge
for perhaps a very long time.
He wanted to run
away
from this image he had of himself.
The brown socks were a mistake.

He made his way back out
to the hall
again and sat
on the blue chair.
He put his coffee on top of the washing machine.

He pulled the brown socks off
and threw them.

Maybe he'd make some toast.

He felt better now that the brown socks were off.
He was a little cold.
He went to the cupboard where he kept some clothes.
He got a T-shirt and pulled it
over his head.
It said *Hooded Fang*
on the T-shirt.
He liked the colours of the T-shirt,
but it was too small.
He sat back down on the blue chair,
took another sip of coffee.
The shirt felt really small.
He sat for a while trying to see
if the day was going to get any different.
After a time, he got up and pulled
the shirt back off.
He went to the cupboard and put it back
on the shelf.
I should get rid of it, he thought.
He got out another shirt.

He sat in the blue chair, hoping
everything would peel away
from the day
now.

His coffee was not too hot.
He'd been born in September.

It looked overcast outside.
There was wind in the tree out front.
His brown socks were off
and his bare feet felt cool on the tile floor.

But still he felt restless.
He got up and went
to the kitchen
and sat in the kitchen
for a while drinking
coffee. He looked outside.

Soon, the girl came down.
Hi, she said.
Hi, he said.
The girl sat in his lap.
He put his arms around her and settled
his head against her.
She stroked his hair.
You wanna make me coffee? she asked.
He nodded.
He made her coffee every morning.

I'm going to move the dresser onto the landing today,
he said, *is that okay?* He tipped his head up.
She kissed him. *Sure, baby*, she said. She stood.
Went to the counter and opened
a drawer, then closed it.
She wasn't sure of anything yet this morning.
She went back to the table.
She sat across from the boy with her back
to the window.
She remembered sitting here on other mornings.

She probably sat here yesterday morning,
but to tell the truth, she didn't really care
if today was today or anything like that.
History sat for her like a cat on the living room rug.
It would get up and confront her occasionally,
but in general it was a warm presence
she was only vaguely aware of
and glad to be aware of,
but it didn't really make any difference to her.
It looks cold out there, she said, turning her head
enough to look out the window.
I know, he said.

§

Some mornings the girl came
down the stairs like something spit
out of a cloud. She stood
before the boy like some terrible storm
descended from the heavens.
Hello, she said when she saw
the boy. *Hello*, the boy stammered. He wanted to ask
if he knew this terrible grey slab
of storm bearing down on him
but a great lump stopped his words
in his throat.

You don't know me, the girl seemed to be
saying. But I know all about you.

The boy felt afraid.

§

They sat,
side by side,
each in one of the faux leather reclining chairs
the boy had brought out to the porch. They were waiting
for the sun
to set.
Eventually, the last bit of sun dipped
below the horizon,
but the sky stayed light
for a time. It was still possible to make out
birds in the distance.

Once they could no longer see
the birds, they went back
into the house and the boy sat
by the window sunk
in his book.

The girl stood in the kitchen, crying, looking
out the window at the trees
marching one beyond the next
into the dusk,
each alone
but all slowly becoming one,
as darkness slithered into their midst,
like an unseen army
eliminating everything
in sight.

§

Do you think we could move the kitchen
table into the living room? the boy asked.
I think you can do anything
you set your mind to, the girl told him.
The boy wasn't sure
about something. He was always a pretty unsure sort
of fellow, but there was something specific
he wasn't sure about right now. He tried to see
what it was in the girl's eyes.

Sometimes you could tell a thing just by looking
into a person's eyes.
There were things the boy was glad to know.
He felt better when he looked in the girl's eyes.
It was reassuring.
He felt less odd.

The girl's smile crinkled her lips. Her cheeks, too.
She looked happy
in a way
the boy couldn't quite imagine.
He tried to smile back,
but he was afraid
it wasn't working.
He couldn't remember how to make a smile.
It was supper time.
The boy and the girl were sitting
across from each other at the table
with plates
of food. The girl stopped smiling and looked

down
at her food. She was trying
to ascertain where she should insert her fork
in order to pull out a small portion of what was on her plate
so that she could lift it
to her mouth,
part her lips
slightly,
and insert the food
into the moist cavern of her mouth.
When did you first see me? the boy asked.
By now, the girl had chosen
a morsel of food and lifted it
into her mouth.
She had it in her mouth,
with her lips closed over it like she needed to keep it
from escaping.
She didn't chew.
She sat contemplating.
The boy couldn't tell if she was contemplating
what was in her mouth
or what he had just asked her.
He closed his eyes and tried
to stop
thinking.
He could feel the fork
in his hand, the handle
end in his hand,
and the pronged end resting
on the edge
of his plate where no food was.
He could see his fork down there,
even with his eyes closed.

He knew he was seeing it in his imagination,
but it felt very real,
like he was right now looking at his fork
with his open eyes,
even though he could feel the place
where his eyelashes intertwined
from his eyes
being closed.
There was a song in the air.
There was no radio in the kitchen,
and only him and the girl in the kitchen,
and no one singing,
and no cats
had joined them this evening in the kitchen,
and the boy knew he was hearing the song
in his mind.
He tried to name that tune (it was a fun game sometimes)
but in the end he knew
what he was hearing was just

the song of the air.
The song that was always there
in the air.
You just didn't always hear it.

If you closed your eyes and imagined
your fork resting
on your plate,
maybe you would be more prone
to hearing it.

He wanted to ask the girl if she heard it,
but there was already a question hanging

in the air
between them.

The boy wondered
why he didn't hear
that question,
why it didn't interfere
with the song in the air,
the song he was following now into sleep.

He pictured the girl. He didn't want to
open his eyes
right now and he didn't want
to ask the girl another question
without first looking into her eyes.

He tried to picture the girl's eyes
in his imagination, but he wasn't sure
if what he saw
pictured was anything
like what
the girl could actually hold
in her eyes.

§

The boy put a kitchen chair in the branches
of the tree in the middle
of the yard
behind the house. *Don't try to sit
in that chair*, he told the girl.

The next day there were two
kitchen chairs in the branches
of the tree and the boy
was lying
in the grass at the base of the tree
with a book draped
over his face.

§

The girl sat on a red plastic chair
in the designated waiting area
of the office
she'd been instructed to go to after
she'd sent in the form. Her feet were wet
from the snow that had gotten in
over the tops of her boots
on her walk from the subway station.

The clerk appeared and asked the girl
to follow him. He smiled
at the girl and showed her
the form she had sent. The girl recognized her handwriting
on the form but she didn't recognize the form.
She followed the clerk around the corner and up
some tiled steps. The clerk unlocked a door and led the girl
into a small room. There were file cabinets
along the walls, with electrical panels
between them and papers
stacked in piles on a metal desk
and on the floor around the desk.

The clerk sat in an office chair
behind the desk, which was in the middle
of the room. He put on a pair of glasses. The girl listened
to the ticking
of a clock that was on the wall
behind the clerk. She watched
the hands of the clock move as the clerk shuffled
through some papers. The clerk asked the girl
some questions but the girl was having trouble
understanding what he was asking
her. She thought she could see the minute
hand of the clock moving and she felt
as though she were moving
with it, in slow motion.

Suddenly, the girl realized the clerk had stopped
asking her questions. He had his glasses
in his hand and he was smiling
at her in a way that made her know he was finished
with her. She got up
and said goodbye.

The clerk is like your angel, the girl told the boy
later that day when she was back
at home. The boy nodded. *I understand*, he said.
He scratched his chin, which was covered
in stubble. He was tired. He had not seen the angel
in what seemed like years.

§

The boy was on the island of floating docks
where they sold the Nikes.
They had very little room to take back any Nikes
in their boat.
It was just a little rowboat with a tiny outboard motor
like the ones for canoes.

The boy was sandwiched between two girls
he didn't know. He talked
with them about something
they shared, as they putted
across the choppy water, in the wind.
The girl he had come with sat quietly
a little further down the boat.

While the others were buying
shoes, the boy went up the hill
to where the old man stood. The old man said, *That's PEI
right there,
my boy.* It was across a narrow waterway
and they could see the steep roofs of some churches
or government buildings
rising above the trees.
The boy slid down the hill, wondering
if he would ever be able to fit in
the boat, but when he got to the bottom
of the hill, he saw
that he was in the attic alone
in the dark with the girl
somewhere deep beneath
calling to him from the bowels
of the house.

§

What the boy noticed
about the girl right away
was her hair.
It was like a spell cast straight out of her head.
It looked like it could move on its own.
Her hair would just wave at him even inside
a room
with no wind.

§

The boy stood
at the top of the stairs,
on the precipice
of this moment.
He could hear the girl in the kitchen frying
something. But he couldn't smell what
it was she was frying.
What was she frying?
He needed to focus.
It wasn't the fact that he couldn't smell
that was worrying him.
He got distracted
too easily.
He needed to make this
happen. He went back
into the bedroom and stripped

the sheets
off his bed.

He could hear the girl
on the phone
now.
She was talking
on the phone.
Do you have all the facts, she said
into the phone.

For a long time,

she said nothing.

She was pacing
around
the kitchen
in her underwear
with the phone
to her ear.

§

It was morning.
They had scheduled the move of the kitchen table
into the living room. It was an auspicious morning,
the boy felt,
for such a move. The weather seemed correct,
if not quite transcendent.

The girl was in his head, in the corner
where she often sat, knitting,
or reading,
or just staring
at the TV. The boy knew
that the girl was still in bed.
He had a brief pang, not exactly
in his heart, but somewhere
in his chest – maybe his heart, since he didn't know
exactly where in his chest
his heart was located – which he interpreted
as a desire to go up and look
at the girl in the bed,
and possibly even touch her
hair gently, but this was the sort of thing he had never done
in all the years they had been together,
and he wasn't about to start now.
He laughed
at himself,
his impulses. He wished the angel would come
and speak to him, but the angel was, as far as he could figure,
erratic.

§

The angel came
at night.

The angel came some nights.

The sound of the angel penetrated the boy
like something roughly forgotten at a moment
when he couldn't remember a thing.

It wasn't as if he was tired.
He wasn't as tired as he sometimes felt.

§

Where's the oven? asked the girl.
She leaned into the gap
in the counter where the oven had been.
The giant outlet where the oven's big black plug had been
was empty.
The floor where the oven had been
was pristine. The boy had cleaned it.
What should we put in there? the girl asked the boy.
She looked up through eyelashes slashed
with sleep.
The desk? the boy pondered.
Where's the stove? the girl asked. She stood
up straight and her nightgown
fell like ribbons.
In the spare bedroom, said the boy.
But you can't plug it in up there, said the girl. *It's got that giant
five-pronged plug.*
That's okay, said the boy, *I'm just storing files in it.*
Oh, said the girl.

§

When the old man returned
that evening, he marvelled
at what the boy had done
with the garage.

Is that your fridge in there? the old man asked.
You didn't buy me a new fridge,
did you? This is only temporary,
you know.
I know, said the boy. It was already November.
The sun shone
into the boy's eyes, making the world
less defined, more malleable.
The wind kept changing
everything
around
him.
Even the old man looked beautiful
in the sun
and wind. He looked happy.

That's our fridge, said the boy.

What will you do for a fridge? the old man asked.

The boy was already far away. He made it known
to the old man that he was far away by walking
away, by putting some distance between himself
and the old man,
as if to say, this bit of distance

between us
is a metaphor for the cognitive distance
I've now placed between us.

The old man watched the boy back away.
He wanted to say something more.
He didn't look so happy now,
but the boy didn't notice.
The boy stumbled a bit at the end
of the driveway, where the asphalt dropped
away from the curb and there was a little lip
of concrete.
The boy turned
and walked down
the road. The old man watched. He shook
his head and went
into the garage. I'll stay
a few months, he told himself. They're going
to need a fridge.

§

I hate that point where you have to open your mouth, the boy said.
The girl laughed. *Just open your mouth, sugar*, she said.
It made him hungry when she called him *sugar*,
and distracted him,
and she always said it
when he was about to say something he really wanted
to say. When he felt like for once opening
his mouth might somehow turn
out to be worthwhile.

§

The boy was sitting
in the living room
in the dark.
He had the TV remote. He was thinking
about watching
some TV. Maybe get a snack. It was two
in the morning. The boy was thinking
that if he could somehow come to understand how
a certain kind of talk was operating, he would be able
to do that kind of talk.
There was a kind of talk
that was partly a fragment
of his imagination – which didn't mean
that this kind of talk didn't exist,
just that it was a fragment of what existed.

But, also, he knew that he could actually do this kind of talk
he was wanting
to do
without knowing what exactly this kind of talk was going
to wind up looking like
when he did do it.
If he ever did.

§

The boy was falling
into water.

§

I have heard of a certain person
or certain persons talking
in a certain way, the boy told the girl,
and, although this is not exactly the way I want to talk
to you, it is always a perfect way for that person
or those people to talk.
I want a perfect way to talk to you. Not a replica
of talk
these perfect talkers do, but a replication of their relationship
to their talk.

§

While he was getting a peach
out of the fridge, it occurred
to the boy that if he stopped
trying to understand, he might easily
understand.

He stood
in the dark kitchen
with the light of the fridge
glowing
on him like he was a holographic image
from the fridge trying to understand
more clearly what he had just understood so perfectly.
He had the peach in his hand, but so far
he hadn't taken

a bite.
He had his hand on the fridge door, but so far he hadn't closed it
yet.
He was trying
to get closer to being
able to talk
about what he had just understood
about understanding. But he didn't quite understand it.
It was because he was trying too hard
to understand what he'd already understood. So he stopped
trying to understand, and immediately,
as though the fridge had released him,
he closed the fridge door,
took a bite of the peach,
and understood
that not trying to understand could
in itself be a kind of understanding.

Oh, I see, thought the boy.
Understanding isn't serial. It's immediate
and complete
at the moment it arrives.
It doesn't arrive in increments,
it arrives complete, and then,
only when you grasp out at it and try to hold on, does it fall
apart
into
increments.

Then,
you spend the rest of your life trying
to put those increments back

together
again. Like you dropped your mom's heirloom
teacup and spent the rest of your life trying
to get the pieces back the way they were before
you dropped it.

It seemed sad, to the boy,
but unavoidable.
He ate the peach, washed his hands, and went back
to sit on the couch
with the TV clicker in his hand.

Eventually the girl got up and found him
sitting there still in the living room with the TV clicker
in his hand and the TV
still not on.

§

They looked together straight ahead out the front of the car
and neither of them moved their heads.
They would not leave the car.
It was cold outside.
But inside the car it was warm. And he was wearing a brown
coat. And a hat (to keep his ears warm).
Her coat was white and bulky and also very warm.
This might have been a sad moment, but it wasn't.
It wasn't a happy moment either.
It was just… (falling slowly here into the world)…

a moment.

It was one of the few moments

they had ever gathered
to them, where they managed
to exist
together with no hopes, no fears, no disappointments, no
desires.
They were both waiting to hear what might happen
next.

§

So I said to Dad, Fuck off, Dad.
The girl watched
the words come
out of the boy's mouth like animals
emerging from a cave, blinking
into the light.
And Dad looked at me, the boy said.
He was standing at the top of the stairs.
We had this sort of circular stairway
in the middle of the house we lived in
back then, going from the front hall
up to the bedrooms on the second floor.
And Dad stood there at the top
of that stairway, not saying
anything, looking
down at me standing in the vestibule. And then,

after a while, he went
into his bedroom and he didn't talk to me
for a year after
that.

§

The boy was keeping his bike
in the tub.

Just for now, he told the girl.
It's temporary, he assured her.

Mornings, the girl went to her mom's
to shower, then came home
to dry her hair
while the boy sat in the kitchen eating
toast and singing
a new song he'd heard
in the air
that morning.

§

The old man peed
in a chamber
pot, then went
and opened the fridge.
There was some beer in it.
The old man laughed.
Closed the fridge.
He wanted one of the beers. He had no idea why. He sat
in the green corduroy chair at the back of the garage.
There was a lamp by the chair, plugged in
to a power bar that was mounted on the back wall

of the garage, and the old man reached back and pulled
the little chain that turned it on.
There was a wicker magazine rack beside the chair
with a few magazines
in it. The old man pulled out a *New Yorker*.
He could hear the girl's small footfalls in the kitchen above
him. It seemed as though she were turning
circles up there.

§

The boy was pulling back
from everything. *For a while now everything has been
possible*, he said.
I don't want to go too far, he told the girl.
He looked up
at the girl.
I should be visible, he said, *at the very end
of vision. But I never quite show myself,
do I?*
No, said the girl, *but this can be lovely
in its way.*

*That drifting can be lovely
for a while.*

§

When I say now, the boy told the girl – *the* now *of when*
I am talking to you – *that now is a now of before.*
The girl was looking
through the window, down the street, but in the corner
of her eye she could see the toast
on the plate in front of her as the boy spoke.
The boy held his toast in his hand. He was looking
at the girl. The boy has made toast again
for dinner, the girl told herself. She looked down
at her toast.
When I say that the now I am talking about is a now
of before, I mean it is a now of before now. I mean I am
in a now that dwells in the now
of before. Do you understand?
No, said the girl,
and the boy nodded,
as though this was the answer
he had been hoping for
all along.

§

After he wrote,
The stubble on the old man's face,
he had nothing.

And he knew it.

§

The boy was standing at the kitchen counter eating
toast. The girl watched
in amazement. The boy spread strawberry jam carefully
across the surface
of his toast. He cut the toast
in half
at an angle
and then again
in half
corner to corner
making four tiny triangles.
The girl had never seen toast
cut like that
before.

The girl's mother had always cut her toast
into rectangles
and then into squares.

When the girl first saw the boy
cut his toast
into triangles, she felt
she was witnessing a miracle.

Later, though,
it bothered her
a little
that all the boy
seemed to eat
was toast.
He ate it quickly.
He would take a bite
and chew

on it
briefly,
and then,
before he even swallowed,
he would take another bite.
He would do this
until he had devoured half the toast,
then he would rub his hands
together
over the plate
so the crumbs showered
off.

You always cut your toast in triangles, the girl told him,
her eyes growing
incredulous.
The boy looked at his toast. They'd had this
conversation a number of times.
The boy picked up one of the tiny triangles
and took
a bite.
Do you ever eat anything
but toast? the girl asked.
The boy held what was left of the triangle in the air
like a wand and nodded
his head. *You know I do,*
he said.
I've never seen you eat
anything but toast, the girl told him.
Really? the boy asked.
Really. The girl tried to look disgusted
but she looked more like someone
who had given up. The girl was wearing rubber boots.

Disgust tends to be a fairly subjective offering.
It often goes unnoticed.

You should eat something, the boy said. *You want some toast?*
He grabbed a bag
of bread and held it up.
The girl did want
some toast.
She wanted
some toast
very badly.
For weeks, now, she had wanted
some toast.
She had been watching the boy
eat toast.
Where do you get all the bread? she asked now.
I never see you leave here.
I've got a bunch of loaves in the freezer, the boy told her.
There's a freezer? the girl asked.
In the basement, the boy said.
We don't have to always eat here, the girl said. *We could go out.*
I like to eat here, the boy said.

§

Last night I had a dream, the boy told the girl. *In the dream, Dad was almost dead. He was still conscious, but he could hardly get out of bed. But he got up anyway and he got out his saxophone and he played a solo.*

I couldn't believe he was doing it,
but somehow it seemed right.
It seemed like it would kill him.
But it seemed right.
He was holding the notes
too long. There was no way
he could have that much breath left
in him
to do that.

After he stopped
playing
he collapsed.
He lay on his back on the floor.

There, *he said, without opening his eyes.*

§

There is this constant hum
that I hear from the heater, the boy thought,
and the odd car horn in the street,
but otherwise there is only ever silence.

§

Days of inaction coalesced
into a kind of hope. Not hope
for some particular outcome,

but hope
nonetheless,
like a spark
of light
that flickers
out
and reignites
then moves
slowly along
unerringly into the future.

§

So the boy went away into the world.
He thought he wanted to be in the world.
He thought he wanted to be alone.
But when he got himself
out there, he faltered.
He hadn't expected to see anyone so far out
from where he started. Part of why he had gone
so far was to get away.
He wanted to slip
through space
and find
himself
with a piece of the world
that was his

alone.

The hard part, the boy thought, is how to be cool and still be able to do what you know has to be done.

§

The boy asked the angel to deliver a message:
I have no real desire
to have you hear from me, Dad. When I think
of you hearing
from me, I think of sections.
I think of things cut into pieces.
I think of things cut in half,
and then cut in half again.

And then cut in half
again. And then cut
in half
again.

That's how I think of things
when I think of you thinking of me thinking
of things.

What I am thinking is something
I can't think
of trusting you
to think of.

§

The girl would contact the aliens eventually.
She would have the boy returned.
(The aliens didn't want him, anyway.)

§

The boy got under the car to take a look.
What the hell
was going on?
It was dark under there.
The boy needed a flashlight.
He got in the car,
turned the key.
Nothing. He reached into his back pocket,
but the note from the girl was gone.
Just the hard press of his ass
against his jeans, and nothing in between.

At sunrise, he walked.
He had intended to drive.
It was cloudy.
The sun never rose that day.
Just this insidious light
limning the boy's eyes.
God's feckless sky
overturned above him.

§

It has to do with the rigid motion of light
splashed up against the fluid unpredictability of sky.
The cops had this guy pulled over for speeding.
The boy was riding
his bike when he saw what
was happening
up ahead.
What if the guy pulls a gun? the boy thought.
He pedalled harder.
He kept an eye on the back of the guy's head.
The cop was in his car, writing up the ticket,
the warm convex currents of air rising up
from the dashboard heater
to meet his fingers
where they wrapped around the pen.

§

The girl discovered one of the boy's poems in the oven
one morning when she went to bake some coffee cake
that she'd mixed for a while at the counter while singing
to the songs on the radio she had perched
on the top of the fridge.
The poem was called 'B is for Big Deal, Q is for Up'

Friends of Marty
went over the falls,
and they all seemed lovable,
so distant and wet.

Their hair did what hair does
in wind
till heads slipped
round the corner

– and gone!

I heard my heartbeat.

§

The girl understood
how the boy's stories dispersed
into a kind of aerosol that she could spray
around the house when she felt her life spiralling into a story
that seemed to have no end.

§

There was a piece of banana bread on the floor of the bus.
It must be a piece of banana bread
that the girl made, the boy told himself softly.
It looked so much like the girl's banana bread
lying there on the floor of the bus.

§

The wind blew the curtains into the room.
The girl could see nothing
but the sky and some clouds. She listened
for far-off voices but what she heard was a lawn mower
somewhere
not too far off.
When the lawn mower finally shut off,
the girl heard the rush of car tires
on the street below.
Then the lawn mower started up again.

§

Sometimes, the boy liked to pretend
that he was typing
on a computer where each letter
that he typed represented
a precious commodity
that he shouldn't squander.
In his mind, he saw himself
spending hours trying to get the words
he wanted
to bend around the words
he already had
so he wouldn't have to delete any letters
that he'd already typed.

§

Everything seemed to pull the boy
further from some destination
he'd set for himself,
a destination he'd sworn lived somewhere
in the music
he'd heard
coming from the garage.
And every minuscule space between the notes
was like a settling
of accounts,
till the boy knew for certain
that getting home required the cessation
of every sound,
musical or not,
and every resurrection of sound
the music accomplished –
the voice of the waitress,
the clink of glass at the bar –
served only one purpose
which was to prepare
him for the terrible
silence of his own return.

§

It was midnight.
Someone had died
down the road
from where the boy was sleeping
tonight. The boy didn't know who had died.

§

Snow fell on the girl's upturned face as she stood
by the shed shedding tears.
Her face was the moon in a sky of pure white,
a doll hanging from clouds.
The sky fell in grey shards.
One white cloud hurried by,
lost.

§

The boy had seen someone
who looked a lot like the old man once before.
Someone who, strictly speaking, must
in fact have been the old man.
But, in every important sense,
the person the boy had seen was not the old man
at all.

§

For months, the candy-assed south wind had had its way
with the boy,
gently wafting
him away,
wallowing in its own humid perspicuity,
insinuating its flatulent arrogance into every crevice

of his life.
But now
it seemed the south wind's dominance was at an end!

§

The girl woke up and the angel was sitting
on the end of the bed.
And she told the girl, *Hush, girl.*
And the girl slept
and when she woke
the angel was gone.
All that was left was a streak
of sunlight that came
through a crack in the curtains
of the girl's hurt eyes.

§

What is that? the boy asked.
The girl was humming a tune.
The boy looked
at the girl.
The girl wasn't there.
It was just the tune.

The boy was alone.

He began to believe he didn't want
to be alone.
He even suspected he couldn't
be alone. It scared him. It was hard. When he saw the girl
for the first time
in a long time
he felt relieved.

For a moment, as he held her, her eyes stayed closed,
but they fluttered
like butterflies
and he saw
a gentleness under the eyelids he had never seen
before. His mind drifted
over thoughts
like cats' paws
choosing spots
on damp lawns
at midnight.

The girl stood up. There was dry grass
in her hair, sticking out
at odd angles,
and more grass stuck
to her clothes.
She looked fierce
and unkempt.

She seemed to be in some sort of walking coma.
At least it took his mind off his loneliness.
He tried to think what he could do for a girl
in a coma.

When he first saw her mouth
it was slightly
open
and her eyes
were slightly glazed
and he might have been afraid
had he not seen her
chest moving.

He had been in his home, eating
something, when he suddenly found himself
in another place …

… this place.

§

The boy was a possible answer
to the questions the girl posed.

The boy filled the girl with answers
that opened the girl further
to the questions
no one ever asked.

§

The boy went out to the mud room
to check his mail tray. On his way back

through the kitchen, he met the girl. *Good morning,*
he said. *Good morning,* the girl said
back. Like they hadn't already
said *Good morning* that morning. It made the girl
nervous, knowing she'd already said good morning
to the boy.
She wondered if he remembered
anything
anymore.

She sat now in the kitchen, which was yellow,
mostly, and the light, if you stayed
in the kitchen too long
could make you nauseous.
The light in the kitchen, the girl thought, is like light
that has forgotten
what it is to be light.

§

The boy and the girl were standing
at the window together looking
out across the yard. The boy had just cleaned
all the windows.
It's beautiful, said the girl.
I used newspaper, said the boy.
It's beautiful, the girl said again.
Thanks, said the boy. He felt he had to head
the girl off, save her somehow from something
he couldn't quite identify,
something that orbited the house

like a tiny satellite.
It's beautiful. This time the girl whispered
it like she was losing track
of her thoughts, trying
to capture something in words
that had no power
over anything
anymore.
The boy smiled, put his arm
around the girl, gripped
her shoulder gently,
pulled her to him.
The two of them looked out
across the yard.
It was growing dark.
The sunset had been spectacular.
The yard was falling away,
a few millimetres at a time,
claimed relentlessly
by the shrinking horizon.

§

What happened to the old man?
the girl asked
one morning, pushing the end table
out of the way, so she could join the boy
at the bathroom sink. Something
had found its way into the girl's dreams
during the night while the girl fell
forward into an alternate realm,

like an animal climbing a wall
but eventually falling back
into the morning where a boy was brushing
his teeth. The girl twirled her hair
in her fist and tucked it
into a bun behind her head.
I haven't seen the old man
in years, said the boy.
I thought I saw him last week, said the girl,
in the backyard, lying
in a hammock, reading
a book.
The girl looked at the boy. She was sure
she had seen the old man, but she wasn't sure
now where, in what incarnation, on what level.
The silver-grey smell of mist
overwhelmed her. She watched it sift away,
the black pants of the moment,
the backs of the knees unfolding
into the future.

§

Not long after she met the boy,
the girl went to visit
the boy's father.
She sat on the wooden Ikea chair
in the father's house,
across from the boy's father,
who sat on the futon.
The boy's father looked dazed.

Light from the big window lit
his face from the side.
My father wasn't a nice man, the boy's father told the girl.
I wanted to be a better father than my father was.
The girl looked at the father's small eyes.
*I wanted to go somewhere
with my life,* the boy's father told the girl.
What was the boy's father trying to tell her
here? *You don't have to go anywhere,* she told the father,
gently. *You just need to be right here
when the boy comes back from buying the groceries.*

§

Did you know there's fish in there? the boy asked the girl.
The girl nodded. *Yes,* she said. *There have always been fish
in there.* She started to say something
else,
but the boy was no longer paying
attention.

*Probably, people kill both
Christians and Romans,* the boy told the girl.
*It isn't humanly reasonable
to expect otherwise. People cannot hope
without wanting.*

He had no idea how long
he stayed
in that one position.
The girl sat up.

For a time, she seemed not to notice
the boy.
Then,
suddenly,
she looked
at him.
She looked at him directly
in the eye. She seemed so focused
that it frightened the boy. He tried to keep the fear
out of his eyes, but he couldn't.

§

On her way home, the girl saw something
she'd never noticed
before.
She assumed it had always been
there and that she had simply never noticed.
But on second thought, she realized
that nothing about it could possibly be considered simple.
It was like one of those shops in a fantasy
novel that appears
one day
between
two shops
that have always been
side by side with nothing
in between
them and you go
in the shop and meet
someone who sells something

to you that seems very ordinary but winds up
changing the course of your life.

§

What makes words real? the girl asked the boy.
I know the answer to that one, the boy said. *But I don't know
if I can say it properly.*
Too early?
Maybe.
They sat together till the girl remembered what she wanted
to eat for breakfast.
It was the same thing the boy wanted to eat,
so she made enough for him
and they ate
their breakfast in the silence of the morning,
and when the afternoon arrived, the boy went upstairs
and took the drawers
out of the dresser and set them on the bed.
He was tempted to pull something
out of one of the drawers.
There were six of them
and they sat like naked appendages torn from a hollow man.
He stacked them in threes.
He wanted to reach into the top drawer
of the stack closest to him.
But he waited.

The angel came to him a while
later and advised against reaching

into any drawers
just yet.

The angel was a real angel
that the boy could hear.

The boy never saw the angel.
He couldn't tell
the girl what the angel looked like.
He couldn't tell the girl about the angel at all.

The boy thanked the angel
and took her
advice.

§

Fourteen kilometres south of where the girl lived
with the boy, a stadium was being built.
There were cars on all the roads.
Exhaust moved invisibly
from the city out to the country.
Five kilometres from where the girl sat
in her kitchen, a woman sat alone
in her car
in the parking lot
of a medical building
listening to a man talk
on the radio.

The kettle sat on a counter
across the room
from where the girl sat.
It occurred to the girl that the fridge,
the cupboards,
the clock on the wall,
the wallpaper,
everything in the kitchen was holding
its breath, standing still in anticipation,
awaiting an arrival. Nothing
is what it is, the girl thought. Everything is merely
a forewarning of something yet to come.
For a moment, the girl sensed the life
of the boy crawling and twitching through
the darkness somewhere else in the house.

At two in the morning, the girl fell
asleep with her head
on the kitchen table.
While she was sleeping, ten children were killed
in a bus accident in the U.K.
Other children were alive in living rooms
around the world, watching television.
At eleven o'clock, the national news came on.

§

At a commercial, the boy goes
into the bedroom. The girl has her suitcases
shut on the bed. She wants to know

if the boy will help
her with her suitcases.

The boy picks up a suitcase, holds it
for a moment, then lifts another one
off the bed and carries them
both out to the hall. He sets them down
at the top of the stairs.
You want your plants? he calls to the girl, who is still
in the bedroom.
No, she calls back, *you keep them.*
They'll die, the boy says.
The girl doesn't answer.
She is still in the bedroom.
The boy sits down on the bigger of the two
suitcases and waits
for the girl.
You should probably take those plants, the boy calls
after a while.
They're yours. He stands, picks up the suitcases
and carries them
down the stairs. He stays
in the front hall waiting
for the girl, but she doesn't come.
The boy calls her,
but she doesn't answer.
The boy notices an ugly stain on the carpet
by the door. He looks at the walls,
then at the ceiling.
There is an old nineteen-inch TV
on the floor by the boot tray.
The boy plugs it in, turns it

on. An old lady with curlers
in her hair sticks her head
out a door. She looks at a man
on the sidewalk in front of her house, then pulls
her head back in and closes the door.
The girl is coming down the stairs now. She has a cigarette
in her mouth,
unlit, and she stands beside the boy
and the two of them look
at the inside of the unopened front door.

Out in the driveway, the girl opens
the trunk of her car, then walks
around and gets into the driver's seat.
The boy puts the suitcases in the trunk and then steps away
from the car and onto the lawn. The girl backs the car out
of the driveway, into the street.
The boy stands on the lawn and watches
the car till he can't see
it anymore. He goes back
in the house.
The girl is gone, he tells himself. She's left me
with this sadness. This sadness is my new friend
that will hang out with me and we can watch TV
together. This sadness will leave
me sometime, same as the girl. I wonder
what I'll be left with then.

§

The boy woke.
The girl was gone.
The house was empty.
There was his bedside table.
A little lamp. He reached
over, put the light on. There was a plate
with crumbs.

He went
downstairs. The light was on
in the kitchen.
I must have left it on
when I went to bed, the boy thought,
but he couldn't remember
going to bed. Maybe the girl left it
on, he told himself. When did the girl leave?
It could have been a long time ago,
the boy thought. How long had the kitchen light been on?

The boy fixed himself an egg.
He sat at the table.
Something about the table.
He tried to remember,
strained, stared.
Something to do with staring
at a table?
The boy stood up. He had taken two bites
of his egg. He had not yet reached the yolk.
He felt regret. What was he regretting?

The boy went into another room. There were rooms
everywhere. He went to five different rooms.

In the sixth room, it occurred to him
that they might all be the same room.

The boy came again to the table where the egg sat,
still on the plate, with two bites
out of it. The boy sat. Something
about a table. He took the plate
with the egg on it and put it in the sink. He sat down
again at the table. He stared.

He heard voices. Were they voices
in the kitchen? Out in the yard? Were they voices
in his head? He remembered hearing voices
coming from waterfalls and from rain
crashing on pavement.

§

*The sea is green
at night*, the boy whispered
into the dark.

The angel hovered
outside the window like a cone
of light.

*But no one goes to the sea
at night*, the boy heard in a voice
like a low growl
or a purr.

§

The day the girl came
back, the boy was on the front porch looking
up at the clouds. He had never seen such clouds.
They'd been up there for days,
scudding like silent Mack trucks across the heavens.
Every now and then the sun came
out, but mostly everything looked dark.
Once in a while, a little rain fell
for a minute
or two
but mainly it was just the clouds.

The girl parked her car
in the driveway and came
to stand by the boy
on the porch. *What are you looking at?* she asked.
The clouds, the boy said.
The still, damp air enclosed them like a cave.
The girl looked up. *What do you see
up there
in the clouds?* she asked.
I see clouds, said the boy. *Just clouds.*
For a while, neither of them said anything.
Then, at the last minute, the boy said,
And the occasional bird.

§

The girl came back
the following spring. The boy had been planning
a picnic the whole time
she was away. He wanted to have
a picnic with the girl
in the backyard of their house,
but the girl said, *No,*
so they went to the park
at the end of the street.
They took their pillows.
They took the hibachi.
They took the ketchup and the pickle relish.
They put everything in a cooler.
At the last minute, while the girl was upstairs
freshening up, the boy slipped
two beers into the cooler.
They loaded everything into the car.
Do you really think we should take our pillows? the girl asked
when they were settled into the car. She giggled.
To her, it was like they were going on a long trip.
The boy backed the car out of the driveway. He drove
the block and a half to the end
of the street where the steel
guard rail kept cars from driving
into the park.

The park was crowded and the boy
stayed in the car for a long time while the girl stood
by the trunk
watching the blue of the sky melt
into the green of the park.
It was a beautiful evening.
Families were milling

about, kids throwing stale bread
at ducks in the pond.

There were ducks everywhere.
There was duck shit on the grass.
There was no place to put the blanket down.
Here, the girl called. *Over here. This is a good spot.*
The boy went over. Looked. He opened his mouth, drew
in a breath. He shook
his head. He waved
his hand
over the area
the girl had chosen. *Duck shit*, he said.
The girl walked back
up the hill
to the car
to get some Kleenex
to try to clean
up some of the duck shit.
She went to pull a piece of Kleenex out
of the box but then she stopped,
her hand
poised above
the Kleenex box.
She turned to see
the boy still
standing
by the spot she had chosen,
hands on his hips, looking down. He was shaking
his head and talking
to himself.
The girl grabbed the box
of Kleenex and walked

back down the hill, trying
not to step in duck shit along the way.

The girl picked up as much duck shit as she could
with the Kleenex, then carried the soiled Kleenex over
to the green wire garbage receptacle at the edge
of the park. Finally, she spread the blanket
out on the grass. They put their pillows at the end
of the blanket. He brought the cooler down,
and the hibachi, and set them near the blanket.
Then they lay down on the blanket
to have a rest. He put his head down
on his pillow. He lay on his back
for a time, looking up at the sky, then turned over
on his side to look out
over the pond.
All the ducks looked diseased
to the boy. Like they had psoriasis.
A big white swan swam past,
slowly,
with one of its feet in the air
behind it. It was paddling
with one foot. It must be injured, the boy decided.
Then the boy remembered a story.
It was years ago.
The guy who told him the story worked for the parks
department. This was before the boy met the girl.
Now, when he thought back
to that time, it was like thinking of someone else.
The story the parks guy told
him was really not much of a story.
There was a mother
duck and her babies living at the pond

that year and one day the mother duck decided
to take her babies
across the road.
(There was some more park
with a river and a little waterfall
on the other side of the road.)
While they were crossing
the road a guy in a pickup
truck ran them over. He got them all
except for one of the babies.
The one little duckling
that survived swam
around the pond
for a few days, looking for its mother,
then died. The guys from the parks department tried
to help, they fed it and so forth, but it was no use.
The little duckling was doomed.
The boy knew for sure that there was still duck shit
under the blanket, no matter how
much Kleenex the girl used
to try to clean it up. He knew
that some part of his body was squishing duck shit
through the blanket.

§

I rode in a cab once
with my dad, the boy told the girl, *and*
while we were in the cab, I heard him
say, Just love each other.
He said it so you could hardly hear

him,
so quietly
you would have thought what you were hearing was a kind
of silence
inhabited by a mute feeling that was so afraid
of itself that the space it inhabited was exactly no space
at all. Dad was staring
out the side window of the cab, watching
some drama unfold
on the street and,
whereas another might have heard
otherwise, what I heard
was, Just love each other.

§

The girl and the boy both looked up
to try to see
the sky
but the oaks blocked out everything
except for isolated streaks of shifting
blue that managed to penetrate
the foliage.

The oaks were an ever-encasing species
arriving again and again at a place
they had never before arrived at,
beginning their day in darkness, then discovering themselves
again in sunlight. They found themselves
where they had never been
before and where they had never been

before was where they were once, before
they had arrived again at the place
where they were never going to be.
And they were always going to be
nowhere, in the way of trees,
swaying where the wind blows, reaching
in this direction
or that,
straying from the upright
but always arriving back
at a place they had never been,
slightly swaybacked today, older
than they once were, and on their way
again to where they had never been
before.

At some point, a violent wind tore
at the tops of the trees, revealing a swath
of blue that momentarily raised the spirits of the boy
and the girl. But the branches snapped
back, as though angry at being tugged
aside so indecorously, and the small
pool of hope that the boy and the girl
had felt closed over again
like the eye of an animal
closing for the last time
beneath the gaze of its stalker.

§

The girl twirled
three times in the middle
of the kitchen. She needed to shed some feelings
she was having. She knew of the centrifugal principle
from when her grandmother was alive and had taken her
to the laboratory where she was looking
for a cure
for something.

§

It was passing late
by the time I got home,
said the boy, *and I was never*
so glad to be shut
of the world,
to shut the front door
behind me,
fix myself a little snack,
and then fall
into bed and sleep
till I had to get up
to pee
a few hours
later.

§

The trip down had been easy. The trip home, too.
And the music was
strange,
both eerie and beautiful and caustically rich.

§

Mud huts. Glass houses. Ice palaces.
The boy hidden
inside the loop.

He would stay inside
the loop
till God made for him a proper limit.

There was an entryway into the world out there –
the boy had seen it.
A world of homes.
Some not what the boy had ever imagined
that homes could be.
Places in other dimensions.
He had to discount these.
He had to discount as much as he could
in order to gain a sense of order
in this loop.

It is how a person should operate, he knew.
It is how the boy decided he would operate
from here on in.

There would be order.

The boy and the girl sat out
on the porch, with the yellow lightbulb
above their heads,
dousing them in yellow
light. The wind took the trees
and tossed aside their branches
like a warlord skewering babies on a stick.
I'm so hungry tonight, said the girl
into the dark
in front of her
face.
Dark clouds rode over the moon
like hobbled horsemen
cantering to their doom.
The girl admitted to the boy that she felt a bit lonely
around the middle
of the day
some days
when she smelled
the boy's toast cooking
in the kitchen.
Sometimes, she told the boy, *I like to come
out onto the porch
in my snowsuit.*
She admitted to the boy that she was cold sometimes,
even in the summer.
The boy and the girl sat
out on the porch together
with their glasses of wine canted
in light
whenever the moon appeared

from beneath the clouds
as if made from relentless descent.

§

The boy was playing cards
by himself when the girl came
through the door.
What are you doing? the girl
asked. The boy held up the deck of cards to show the girl
what he was doing.
The girl took off her coat and went
into the kitchen. She called to the boy,
asked if he wanted a sandwich. *I could make you
a grilled cheese*, she called.
Sounds good, the boy called back.
The girl pulled open the pot drawer
under the oven. She sat down
on the floor. *Do you know where the fry pans are?* she called.
There's nothing
but a turntable under the oven.
The boy came into the kitchen
doorway and looked at the girl.
He walked over and lifted the turntable out
from under the oven. *I was wondering
where that was*, he said. He went back
into the living room. He tried to remember
where he had put his records.
He set the turntable on the ottoman.
He sat on the couch and put his feet
on the packing crate.

When the girl came out to the living room,
the boy was practicing card tricks. The girl watched
for a while. *You're doing that wrong,* she told the boy.
The boy looked at the girl, then back
at the cards laid out on the packing crate
in front of him. *I've seen that trick,* the girl says.
You're doing it wrong.
The boy scooped up all the cards,
then shuffled them a number of times.
The girl went back to the kitchen.

§

The boy went upstairs to get the girl,
but the girl had decided she would stay
in bed because
she had a bit of a sore throat and she'd sworn upon waking
not to let it get worse
and the boy felt like he had everything to give
the girl.

The boy held the girl awhile
and told her he loved her
and explained
some other stuff
he wanted to say.
He knew that the girl was probably not listening,
just wanting to get back to sleep.
And the boy said only a few words, really.

I want to fall, he said,
and fall,
somewhere,
for a long while,
while I pay for my crimes in speaking
such loneliness
as words always speak.
Beyond the mosaic of yellow squares,
said the boy,
that rise up in the dark like a wall
above my bed, there is another universe,
a world where I fall
into the faces of passers-by, inhabiting them
like a candle
with new light, a new way
for them to touch the world.

But they run off ahead of me,
trailing me behind them
like a vapour trail, or the tail of a kite, luminous
in the sky above. I'm out
again, my own self tipping quietly
toward the yellow wall, wanting always
to go back through,
but there are some days when you just can't.
Sometimes weeks. There might have been a number of years
there when I never remembered
that the yellow wall was there.
Some days you just have to ride the bus
to work and continue to hope.
Or not even that. Forget hope.
Just carry on. Slide along

in faith. Something might matter again
someday.

§

I would like to go to sleep at night, the boy told the girl
most nights
but not always.
Some nights, the boy said, *sleep comes hard.*
Sparkling, the girl held her breasts to herself as her tears fell.
There was something jewel-like about the morning.
I like to go to sleep at night, the boy said, again,
but neither of them heard
anything
but the sound inside of everything.

§

The sun was shining
but the air was cool
and the boy was whistling a tune
as he stepped out onto the porch.
He stood for a time with his hand
still on the screen door, looking at the chairs
where he and the girl sat at night before they gave up
on the day finally and went in
to bed.
I should have had another cup of coffee, the boy said to himself.
I should have brought one out to the yard with me.

He had the newspaper with him
and he was tempted to sit down and take a boo.
I'd better do a bit of yard work
first, though, he thought.
It was sixty-five degrees Fahrenheit.
Perfect for doing yard work.

§

After dinner, the boy and the girl went
into the living room to watch TV. The boy fell
asleep.

Wake up, the girl said.
I'm awake, the boy told her.
It's the part where the little kid gets killed,
the girl said. *I hate this part.*
The boy stared at the TV, blinking. He scratched
his head with both hands. *We've seen this*, he said.
The kid on the TV was talking
softly to a man
who was holding a gun
against the kid's head.

The boy went into the kitchen to get a snack.
Could you get me some water? the girl called.
The boy opened the fridge.
He heard the gun
go off. The girl made a sound,
like she was startled.
The boy got an apple and a glass of water

and went back
out to the living room.
He set the water on the packing crate
they used for a coffee table.
I hope they catch that guy, the girl whispered.
They do, the boy said. *We've seen this.*
The girl looked at the boy, her eyes like cartoons
in the light of the TV.

A commercial came on. *I've got to go
to bed soon,* said the girl. She looked at the boy's
hands. He had a deck of cards
in them. The girl went away,

then came back with her hairbrush.
She stood in front of the TV brushing
her hair. *I just want to see them catch that guy,* she said.
Pick a card, said the boy. He held the cards
out toward the girl.
She picked a card.
Don't show me, said the boy.
The girl held the card tight
against her chest.
She tipped her head down to peek
at the card.
Remember what your card is, the boy said.
The girl nodded.
The boy held the deck of cards toward the girl and gestured
for her to put the card back in. He turned his
head away from the girl
so he wouldn't see
the card when she put it back
in the deck.

Okay, said the girl, *I put it back.*
The boy turned
and looked
at the girl.
He shuffled
the deck.
He cut it four times,
then shuffled
again.
He set the deck down on the table and did a little drum roll
with his fingers on the packing crate.
He fanned the cards across the crate and
pulled out the queen of spades. He showed it
to the girl. *Is that your card?* he asked.
The girl looked.
No, she said. She laughed. *That's not my card*, she said.
She laughed again. *You're an idiot*, she said.
She kissed the boy on the forehead.
She stepped back,
looked down at the boy.
She shook her head,
laughed some more, then went
up to bed.

Books by Ken Sparling

Dad Says He Saw You at the Mall

Hush Up and Listen Stinky Poo Butt

An untitled novel

For Those Whom God Has Blessed with Fingers

Book

Intention Implication Wind

Typeset in Adobe Jenson Pro.

Printed at the old Coach House on bpNichol Lane in Toronto, Ontario, on Zephyr Antique Laid paper, which was manufactured, acid-free, in Saint-Jérôme, Quebec, from second-growth forests. This book was printed with vegetable-based ink on a 1965 Heidelberg KORD offset litho press. Its pages were folded on a Baumfolder, gathered by hand, bound on a Sulby Auto-Minabinda and trimmed on a Polar single-knife cutter.

Edited for the press by Derek McCormack
Cover by Wenting Li

Coach House Books
80 bpNichol Lane
Toronto ON M5S 3J4
Canada

416 979 2217
800 367 6360

mail@chbooks.com
www.chbooks.com